STAR WARS®

THE CLONE WARS™

SLAVES OF THE REPUBLIC
VOLUME THREE
"THE DEPTHS OF ZYGERRIA"

SCRIPT
HENRY GILROY

PENCILS
LUCAS MARANGON

INKS
DAN PARSONS

COLORS
MICHAEL E. WIGGAM

LETTERING
MICHAEL HEISLER

COVER ART
LUCAS MARANGON

The search continues! Following an invasion by Count Dooku's droid army, the Togruta people of the colony Kiros mysteriously disappeared. Jedi Knights Anakin and Obi-Wan, and Padawan Ahsoka, are on the trail of the planet's vanished population. The trail leads to Zygerrian slavers, and the Jedi track down a faction of the crimson-haired villains in the black-market debris field known as the Shi'Kar Straits.

After a fierce battle with cunning Captain Onyx and his cutthroat crew, the Jedi board the villain's vessel and take control. Upon interrogating Onyx, the Jedi discover the Zygerrians are soon to host a grand slave auction involving the missing Togruta.

Intending to infiltrate the auction so that they can rescue the Togruta, the Jedi commandeer a slaver vessel, *Fate's Hand*, and journey into enemy territory . . .

DARK HORSE COMICS

Spotlight

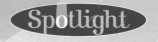

VISIT US AT
www.abdopublishing.com

Reinforced library bound edition published in 2010 by Spotlight, a division of the ABDO Group, 8000 West 78th Street, Edina, Minnesota 55439. Spotlight produces high-quality reinforced library bound editions for schools and libraries. Published by agreement with Dark Horse Comics, Inc., and Lucasfilm Ltd.

Printed in the United States of America, Melrose Park, Illinois.
092009
012010

 PRINTED ON RECYCLED PAPER

Library of Congress Cataloging-in-Publication Data

Gilroy, Henry.
   Slaves of the republic / script by Henry Gilroy ; pencils by Scott Hepburn ; inks by Dan Parsons ; colors by Michael E. Wiggam ; lettering by Michael Heisler.
-- Reinforced library bound ed.
      v. cm. -- (Star wars: the clone wars)
   "Dark Horse Comics."
   Contents: v. 1. The mystery of Kiros -- v. 2. Slave traders of Zygerria -- v. 3. The depths of Zygerria -- v. 4. Auction of a million souls -- v. 5. A slave now, a slave forever -- v. 6. Escape from kadavo.
   ISBN 978-1-59961-710-7 (v. 1) -- ISBN 978-1-59961-711-4 (v. 2) -- ISBN 978-1-59961-712-1 (v. 3) -- ISBN 978-1-59961-713-8 (v. 4) -- ISBN 978-1-59961-714-5 (v. 5) -- ISBN 978-1-59961-715-2 (v. 6)
   1. Graphic novels. [1. Graphic novels.] I. Hepburn, Scott. II. Star Wars, the clone wars (Television program) III. Title.
   PZ7.7.G55Sl 2010
   [Fic]--dc22
                                        2009030553

All Spotlight books have reinforced library bindings and
are manufactured in the United States of America.

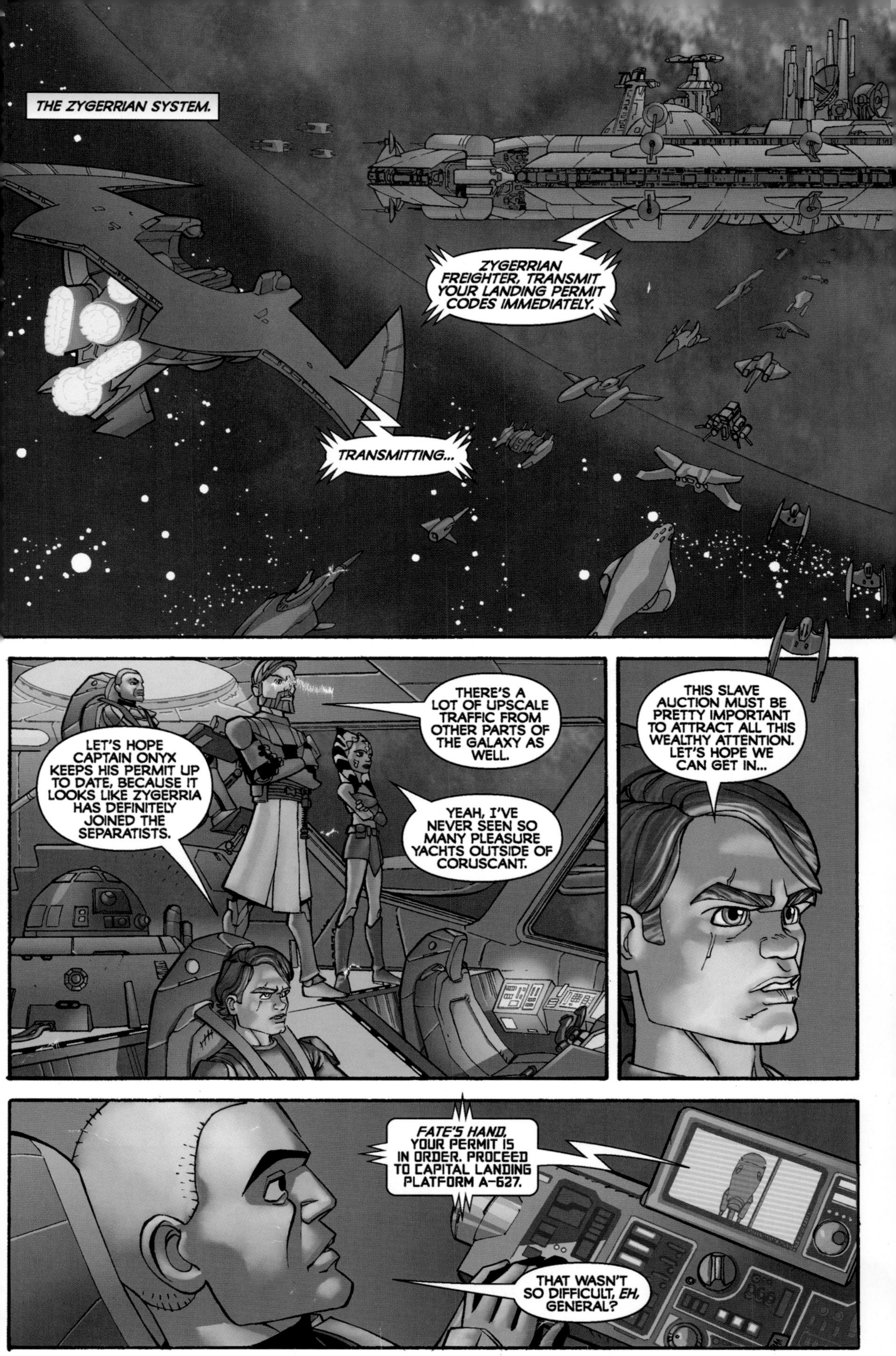
THE ZYGERRIAN SYSTEM.
ZYGERRIAN FREIGHTER, TRANSMIT YOUR LANDING PERMIT CODES IMMEDIATELY.
TRANSMITTING...
THERE'S A LOT OF UPSCALE TRAFFIC FROM OTHER PARTS OF THE GALAXY AS WELL.
LET'S HOPE CAPTAIN ONYX KEEPS HIS PERMIT UP TO DATE, BECAUSE IT LOOKS LIKE ZYGERRIA HAS DEFINITELY JOINED THE SEPARATISTS.
YEAH, I'VE NEVER SEEN SO MANY PLEASURE YACHTS OUTSIDE OF CORUSCANT.
THIS SLAVE AUCTION MUST BE PRETTY IMPORTANT TO ATTRACT ALL THIS WEALTHY ATTENTION. LET'S HOPE WE CAN GET IN...
FATE'S HAND, YOUR PERMIT IS IN ORDER. PROCEED TO CAPITAL LANDING PLATFORM A-627.
THAT WASN'T SO DIFFICULT, *EH*, GENERAL?

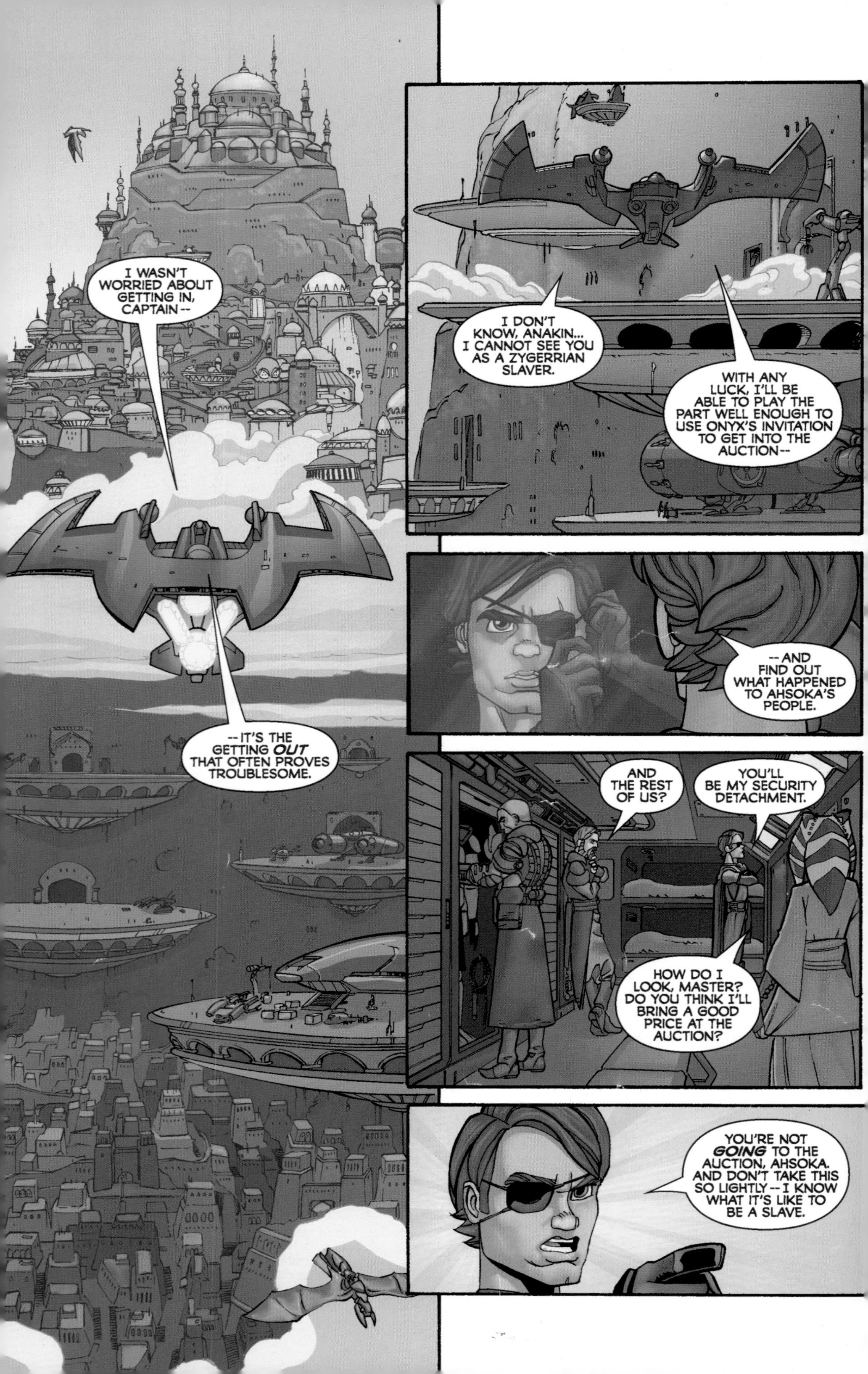
I WASN'T WORRIED ABOUT GETTING IN, CAPTAIN--
--IT'S THE GETTING *OUT* THAT OFTEN PROVES TROUBLESOME.
I DON'T KNOW, ANAKIN... I CANNOT SEE YOU AS A ZYGERRIAN SLAVER.
WITH ANY LUCK, I'LL BE ABLE TO PLAY THE PART WELL ENOUGH TO USE ONYX'S INVITATION TO GET INTO THE AUCTION--
--AND FIND OUT WHAT HAPPENED TO AHSOKA'S PEOPLE.
AND THE REST OF US?
YOU'LL BE MY SECURITY DETACHMENT.
HOW DO I LOOK, MASTER? DO YOU THINK I'LL BRING A GOOD PRICE AT THE AUCTION?
YOU'RE NOT *GOING* TO THE AUCTION, AHSOKA. AND DON'T TAKE THIS SO LIGHTLY-- I KNOW WHAT IT'S LIKE TO BE A SLAVE.

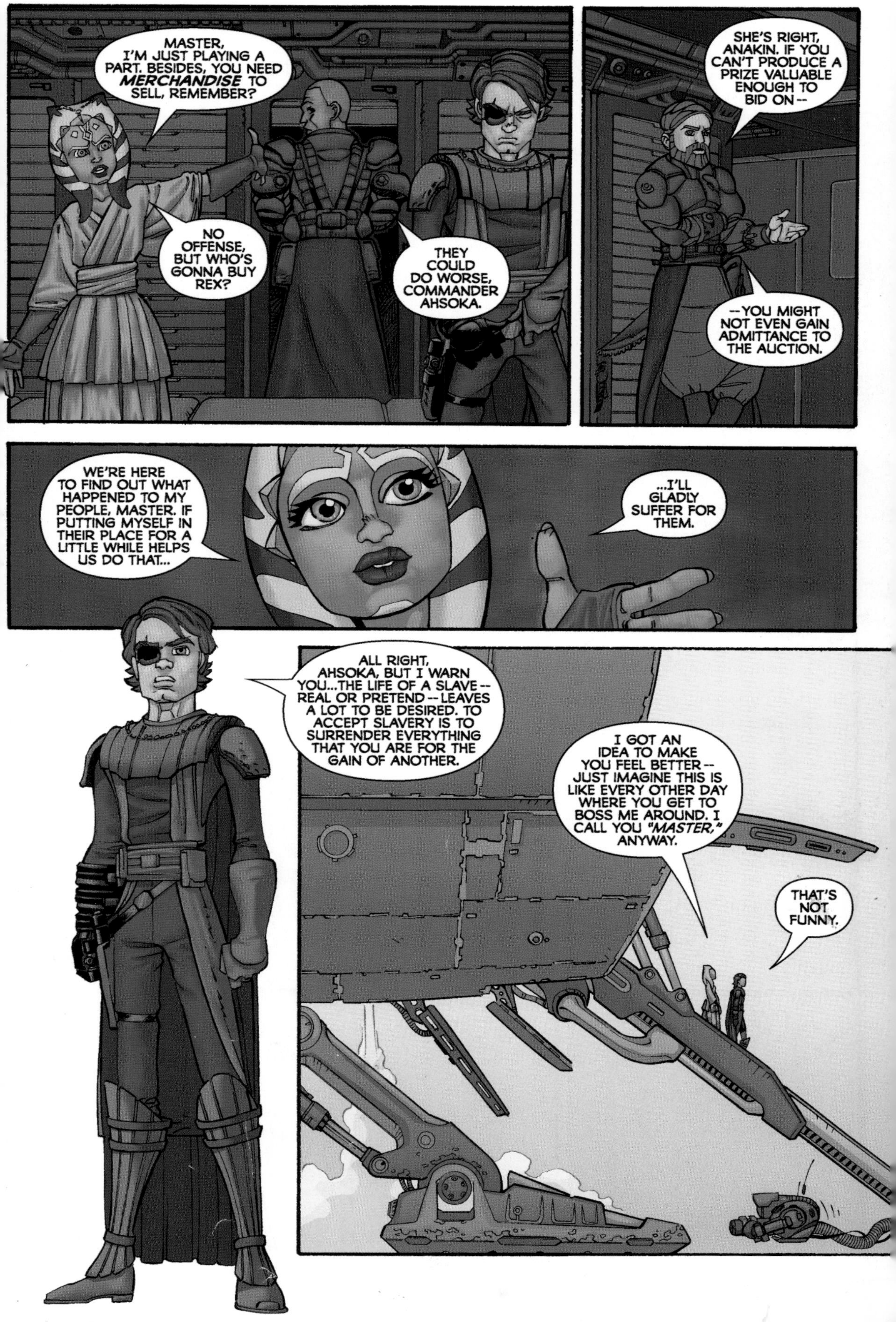

MASTER, I'M JUST PLAYING A PART. BESIDES, YOU NEED *MERCHANDISE* TO SELL, REMEMBER?
NO OFFENSE, BUT WHO'S GONNA BUY REX?
THEY COULD DO WORSE, COMMANDER AHSOKA.
SHE'S RIGHT, ANAKIN. IF YOU CAN'T PRODUCE A PRIZE VALUABLE ENOUGH TO BID ON--
--YOU MIGHT NOT EVEN GAIN ADMITTANCE TO THE AUCTION.
WE'RE HERE TO FIND OUT WHAT HAPPENED TO MY PEOPLE, MASTER. IF PUTTING MYSELF IN THEIR PLACE FOR A LITTLE WHILE HELPS US DO THAT...
...I'LL GLADLY SUFFER FOR THEM.
ALL RIGHT, AHSOKA, BUT I WARN YOU...THE LIFE OF A SLAVE--REAL OR PRETEND--LEAVES A LOT TO BE DESIRED. TO ACCEPT SLAVERY IS TO SURRENDER EVERYTHING THAT YOU ARE FOR THE GAIN OF ANOTHER.
I GOT AN IDEA TO MAKE YOU FEEL BETTER--JUST IMAGINE THIS IS LIKE EVERY OTHER DAY WHERE YOU GET TO BOSS ME AROUND. I CALL YOU *"MASTER,"* ANYWAY.
THAT'S NOT FUNNY.

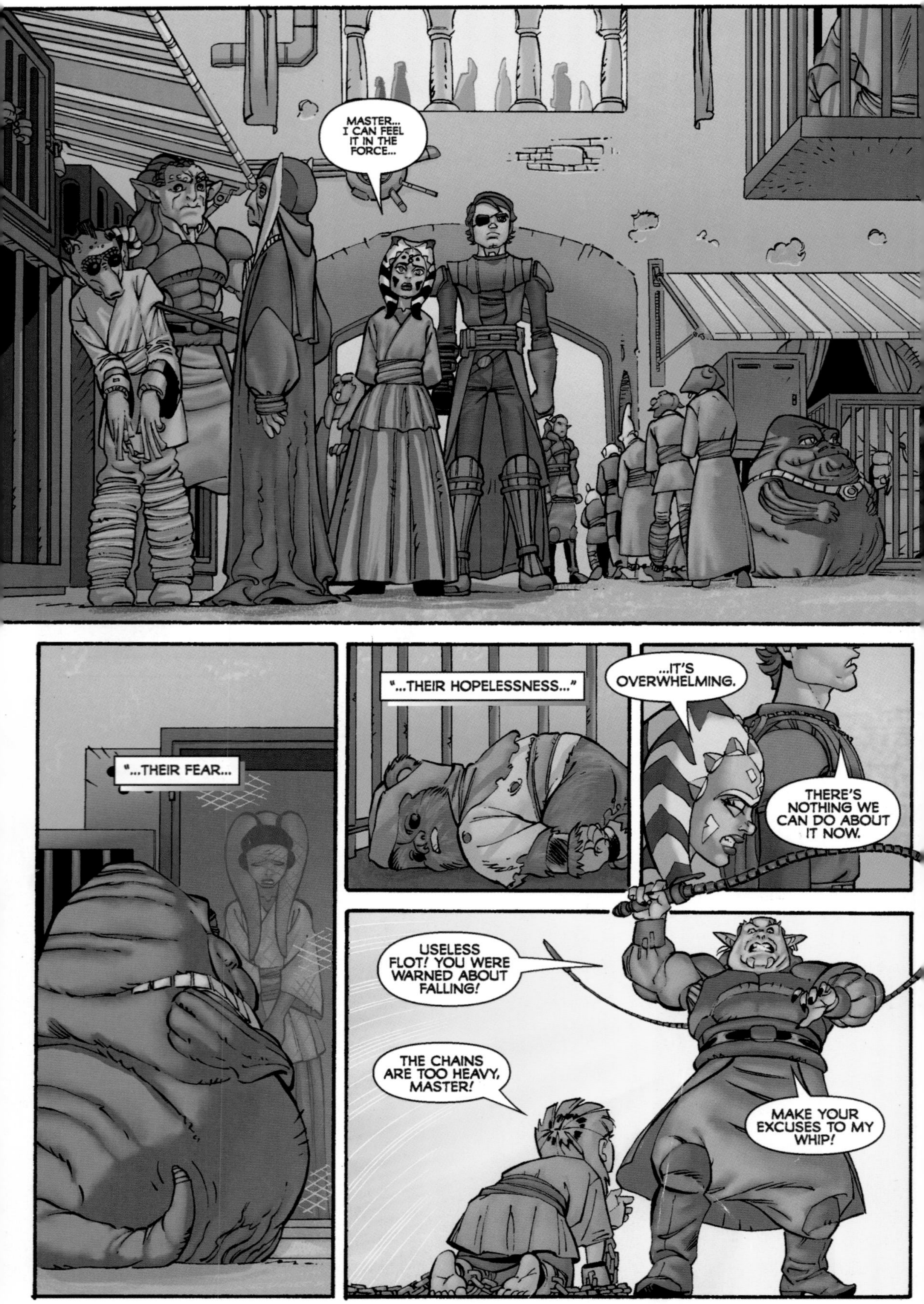
MASTER... I CAN FEEL IT IN THE FORCE...
"...THEIR FEAR...
"...THEIR HOPELESSNESS..."
...IT'S OVERWHELMING.
THERE'S NOTHING WE CAN DO ABOUT IT NOW.
USELESS FLOT! YOU WERE WARNED ABOUT FALLING!
THE CHAINS ARE TOO HEAVY, MASTER!
MAKE YOUR EXCUSES TO MY WHIP!

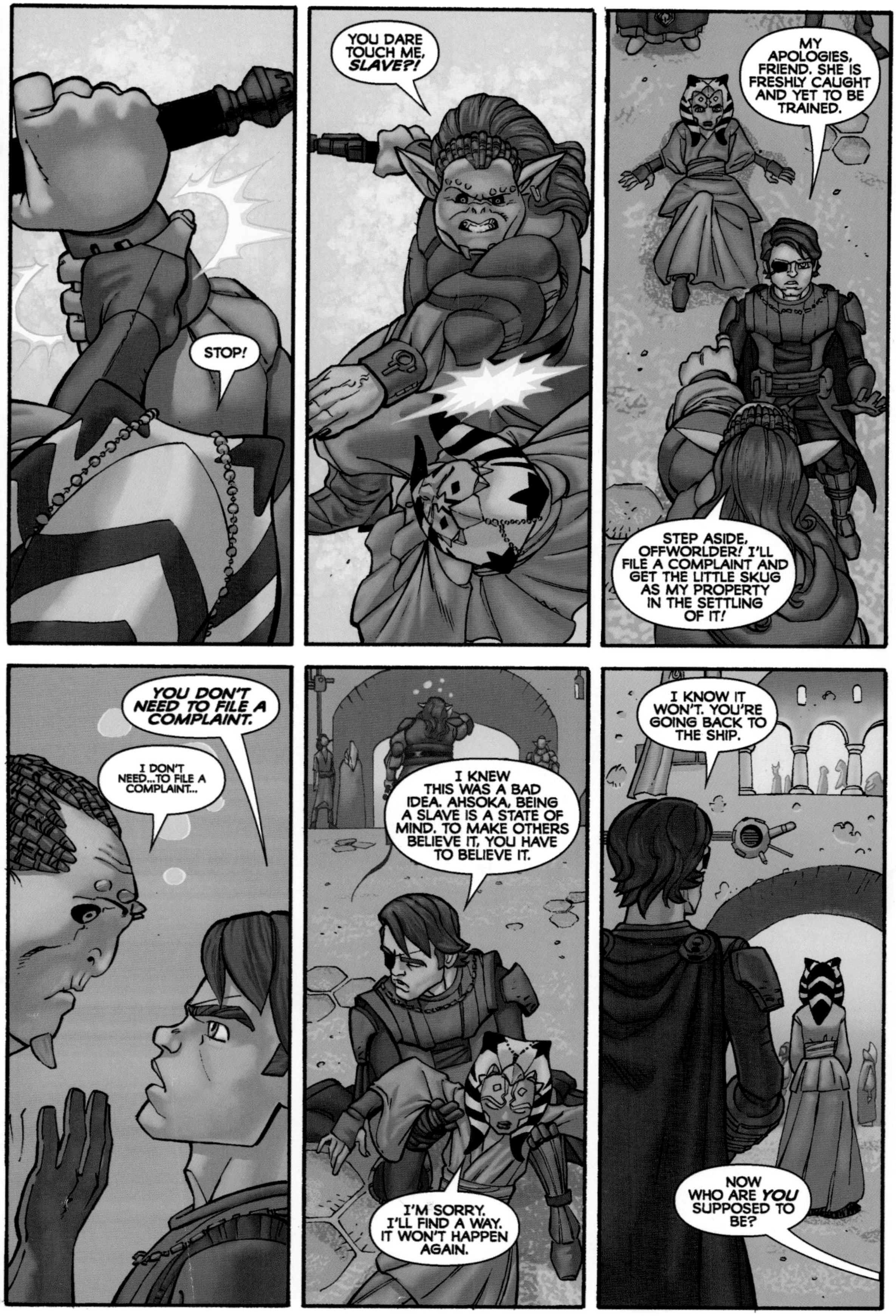
STOP!
YOU DARE TOUCH ME, SLAVE?!
MY APOLOGIES, FRIEND. SHE IS FRESHLY CAUGHT AND YET TO BE TRAINED.
STEP ASIDE, OFFWORLDER! I'LL FILE A COMPLAINT AND GET THE LITTLE SKUG AS MY PROPERTY IN THE SETTLING OF IT!
YOU DON'T NEED TO FILE A COMPLAINT.
I DON'T NEED...TO FILE A COMPLAINT...
I KNEW THIS WAS A BAD IDEA. AHSOKA, BEING A SLAVE IS A STATE OF MIND. TO MAKE OTHERS BELIEVE IT, YOU HAVE TO BELIEVE IT.
I'M SORRY. I'LL FIND A WAY. IT WON'T HAPPEN AGAIN.
I KNOW IT WON'T. YOU'RE GOING BACK TO THE SHIP.
NOW WHO ARE YOU SUPPOSED TO BE?

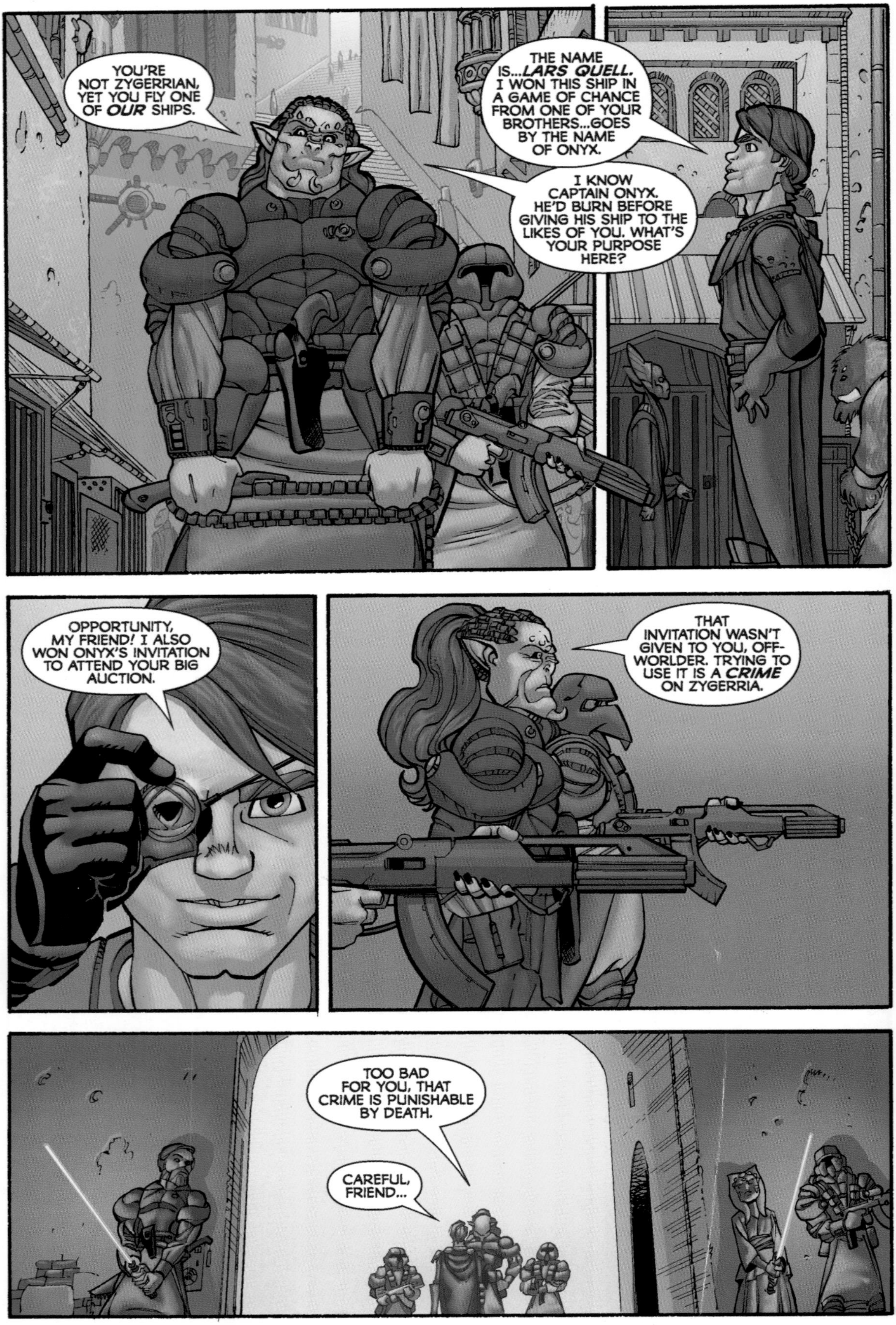
YOU'RE NOT ZYGERRIAN, YET YOU FLY ONE OF *OUR* SHIPS.
THE NAME IS...*LARS QUELL.* I WON THIS SHIP IN A GAME OF CHANCE FROM ONE OF YOUR BROTHERS...GOES BY THE NAME OF ONYX.
I KNOW CAPTAIN ONYX. HE'D BURN BEFORE GIVING HIS SHIP TO THE LIKES OF YOU. WHAT'S YOUR PURPOSE HERE?
OPPORTUNITY, MY FRIEND*!* I ALSO WON ONYX'S INVITATION TO ATTEND YOUR BIG AUCTION.
THAT INVITATION WASN'T GIVEN TO YOU, OFF-WORLDER. TRYING TO USE IT IS A *CRIME* ON ZYGERRIA.
TOO BAD FOR YOU, THAT CRIME IS PUNISHABLE BY DEATH.
CAREFUL, FRIEND...

BDOW!

...I MIGHT BE ABLE TO DRAW FASTER THAN YOU!

YOU'RE FAST, BUT IT WON'T SAVE YOU.

WANT TO BET?

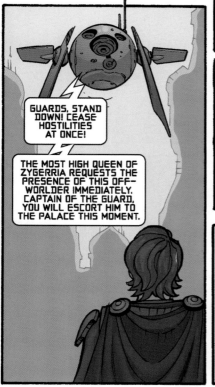

GUARDS, STAND DOWN! CEASE HOSTILITIES AT ONCE!

THE MOST HIGH QUEEN OF ZYGERRIA REQUESTS THE PRESENCE OF THIS OFF-WORLDER IMMEDIATELY. CAPTAIN OF THE GUARD, YOU WILL ESCORT HIM TO THE PALACE THIS MOMENT.

BETTER LUCK NEXT TIME.

IF YOU THINK YOU'RE OUT OF MY REACH, THINK AGAIN. THIS WAY...

TROUBLE SEEMS TO FIND GENERAL SKYWALKER EVERYWHERE HE GOES.

YOU'RE *JUST* NOTICING THAT, CAPTAIN? BETTER LEAVE OUR LIGHTSABERS HERE IN CASE WE RUN INTO SIMILAR TROUBLE.

LOOK AFTER THESE, ARTOO. AND SEAL THE DOOR AFTER WE'RE GONE. WE DON'T WANT ANYONE MAKING A SLAVE OUT OF *YOU.*

BWOOOP...

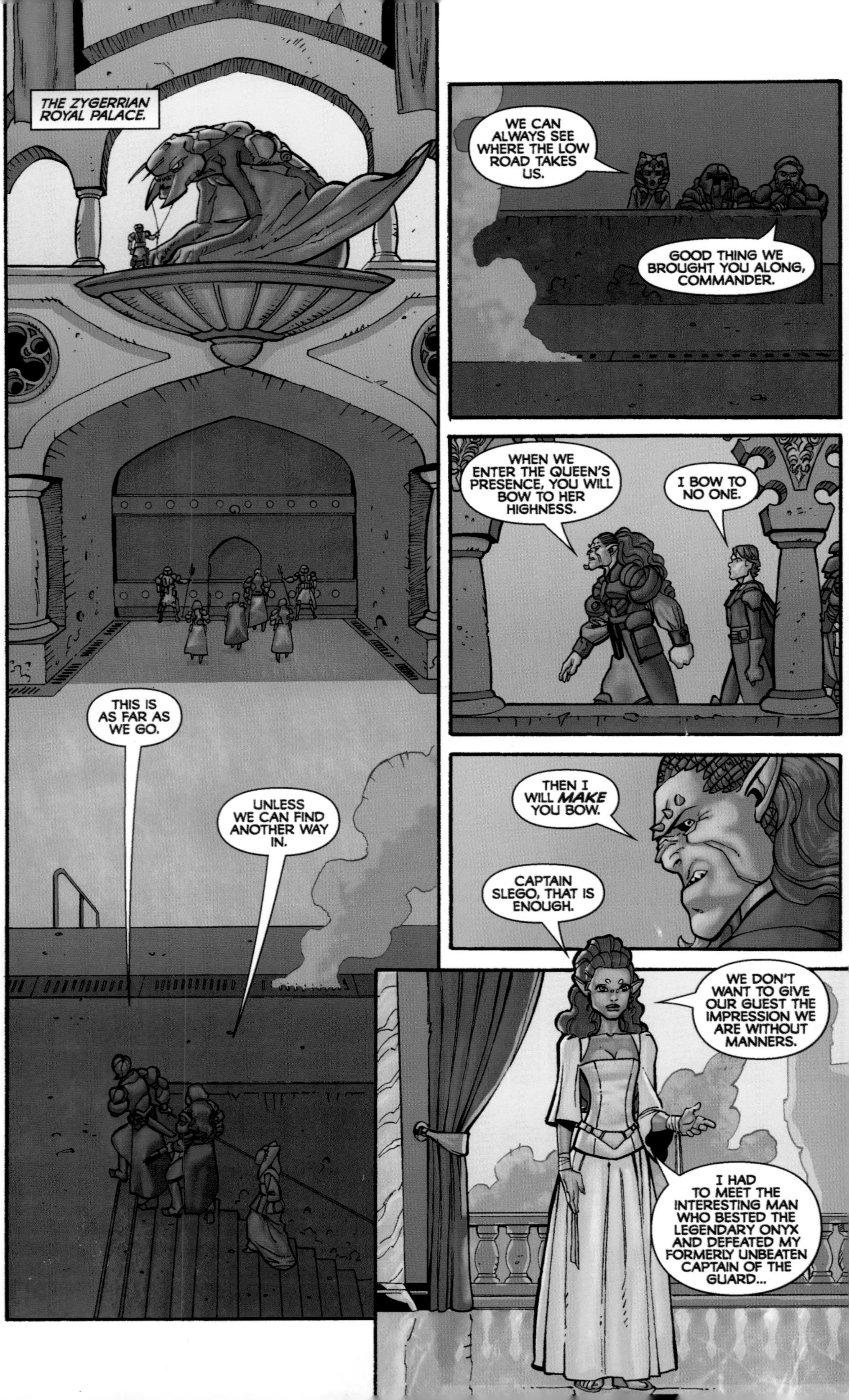
THE ZYGERRIAN ROYAL PALACE.
THIS IS AS FAR AS WE GO.
UNLESS WE CAN FIND ANOTHER WAY IN.
WE CAN ALWAYS SEE WHERE THE LOW ROAD TAKES US.
GOOD THING WE BROUGHT YOU ALONG, COMMANDER.
WHEN WE ENTER THE QUEEN'S PRESENCE, YOU WILL BOW TO HER HIGHNESS.
I BOW TO NO ONE.
THEN I WILL MAKE YOU BOW.
CAPTAIN SLEGO, THAT IS ENOUGH.
WE DON'T WANT TO GIVE OUR GUEST THE IMPRESSION WE ARE WITHOUT MANNERS.
I HAD TO MEET THE INTERESTING MAN WHO BESTED THE LEGENDARY ONYX AND DEFEATED MY FORMERLY UNBEATEN CAPTAIN OF THE GUARD...

...AND WHO IS SO BOLD HE WILL NOT BOW TO ME.

I MEAN NO DISRESPECT, BUT YOU ARE NOT *MY* QUEEN.

NOT *YET*, PERHAPS. LEAVE US, CAPTAIN.

AS YOU WISH.

TELL ME HOW YOU CAME TO MY WORLD, QUELL, IS IT?

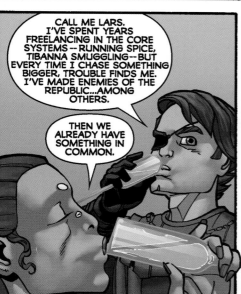

CALL ME LARS. I'VE SPENT YEARS FREELANCING IN THE CORE SYSTEMS -- RUNNING SPICE, TIBANNA SMUGGLING--BUT EVERY TIME I CHASE SOMETHING BIGGER, TROUBLE FINDS ME. I'VE MADE ENEMIES OF THE REPUBLIC...AMONG OTHERS.

THEN WE ALREADY HAVE SOMETHING IN COMMON.

WE SEEK A BETTER LIFE...

...AND THERE ARE MANY WHO WOULD STOP US FROM TAKING IT.

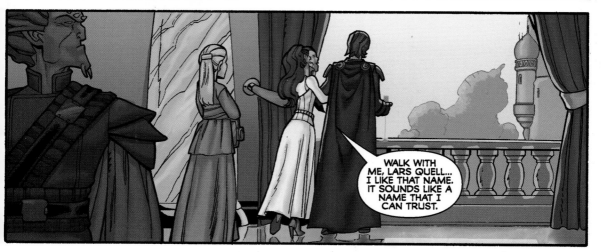

WALK WITH ME, LARS QUELL... I LIKE THAT NAME. IT SOUNDS LIKE A NAME THAT I CAN TRUST.

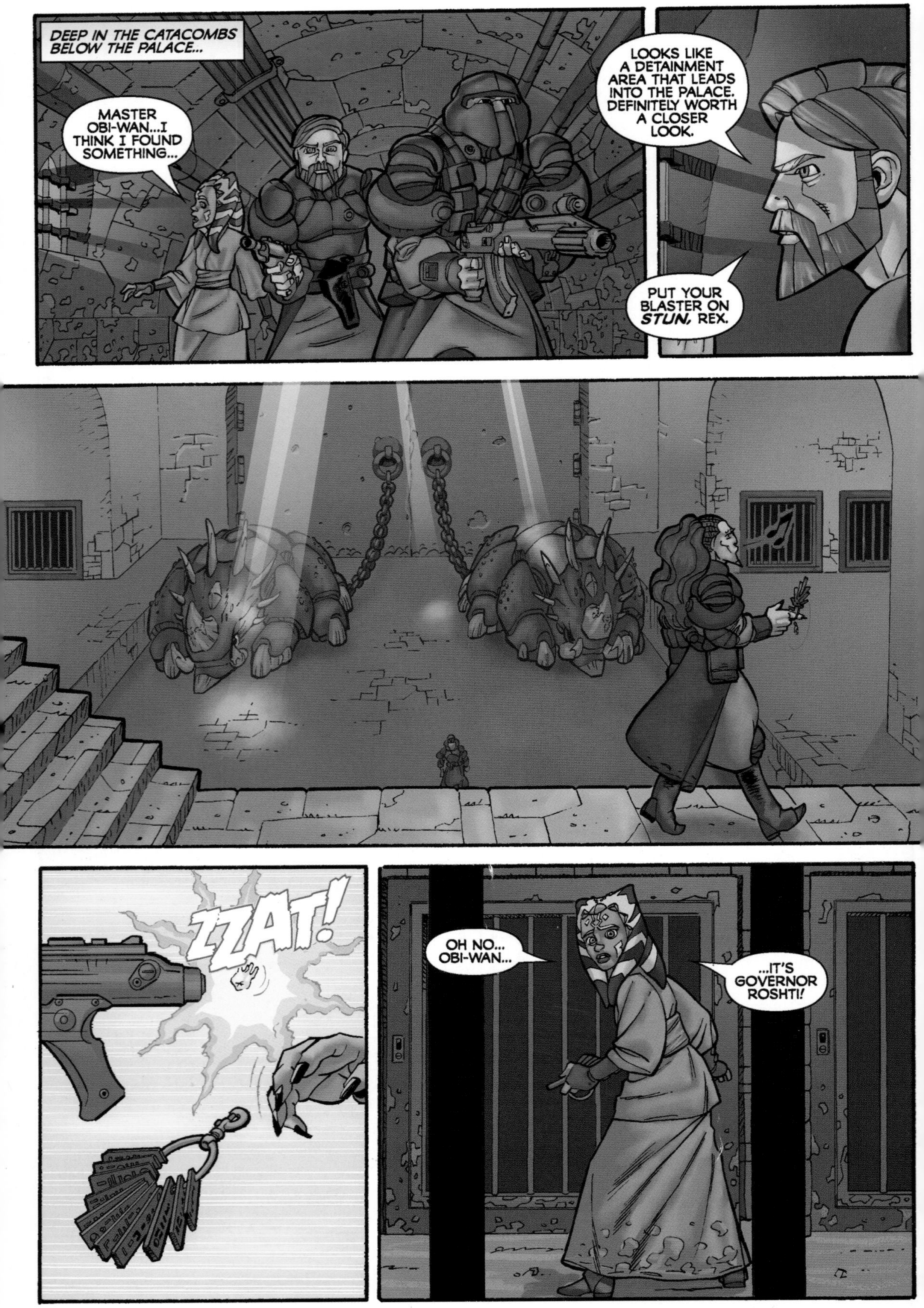
DEEP IN THE CATACOMBS BELOW THE PALACE...
MASTER OBI-WAN...I THINK I FOUND SOMETHING...
LOOKS LIKE A DETAINMENT AREA THAT LEADS INTO THE PALACE. DEFINITELY WORTH A CLOSER LOOK.
PUT YOUR BLASTER ON STUN, REX.
ZZAT!
OH NO... OBI-WAN...
...IT'S GOVERNOR ROSHTI!

DO I... KNOW YOU?

I AM JEDI KNIGHT OBI-WAN KENOBI. WE'RE GOING TO GET YOU OUT OF HERE.

TOO LATE, MASTER JEDI, I HAVE FAILED MY PEOPLE...THEY ARE GONE. WHERE I DO NOT KNOW...

WE'LL FIND THEM, MY LORD. WHATEVER IT TAKES.

INTRUDERS!

AHSOKA, GET ABOARD THIS CREATURE!

WHAT ARE WE DOING?

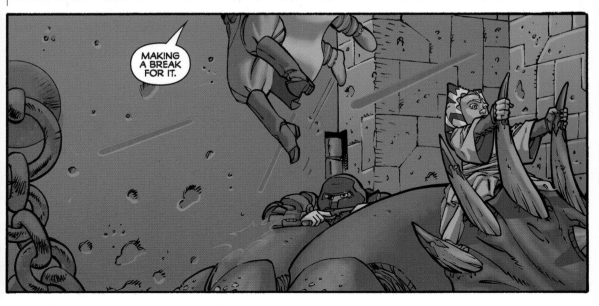

MAKING A BREAK FOR IT.

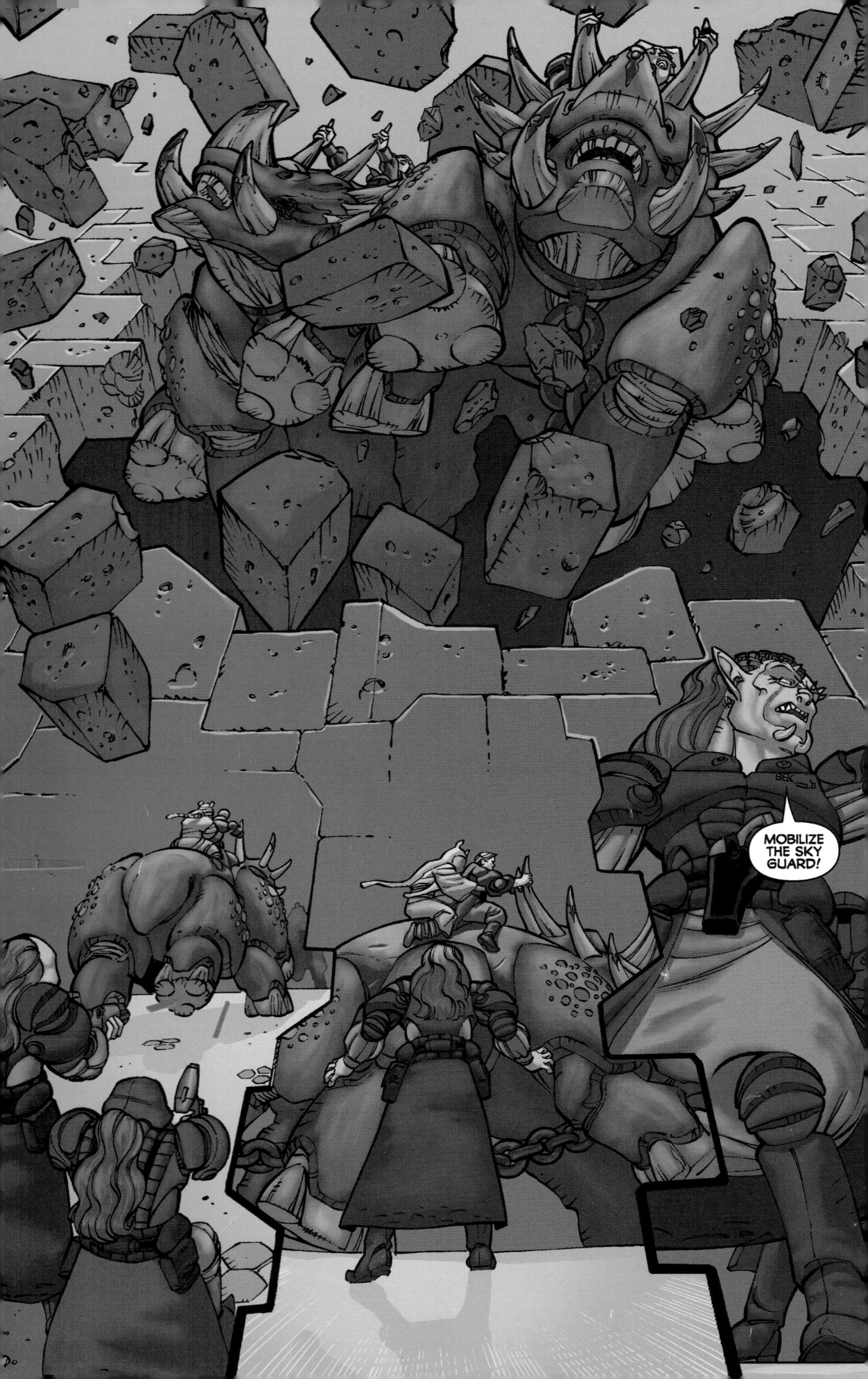
MOBILIZE THE SKY GUARD!

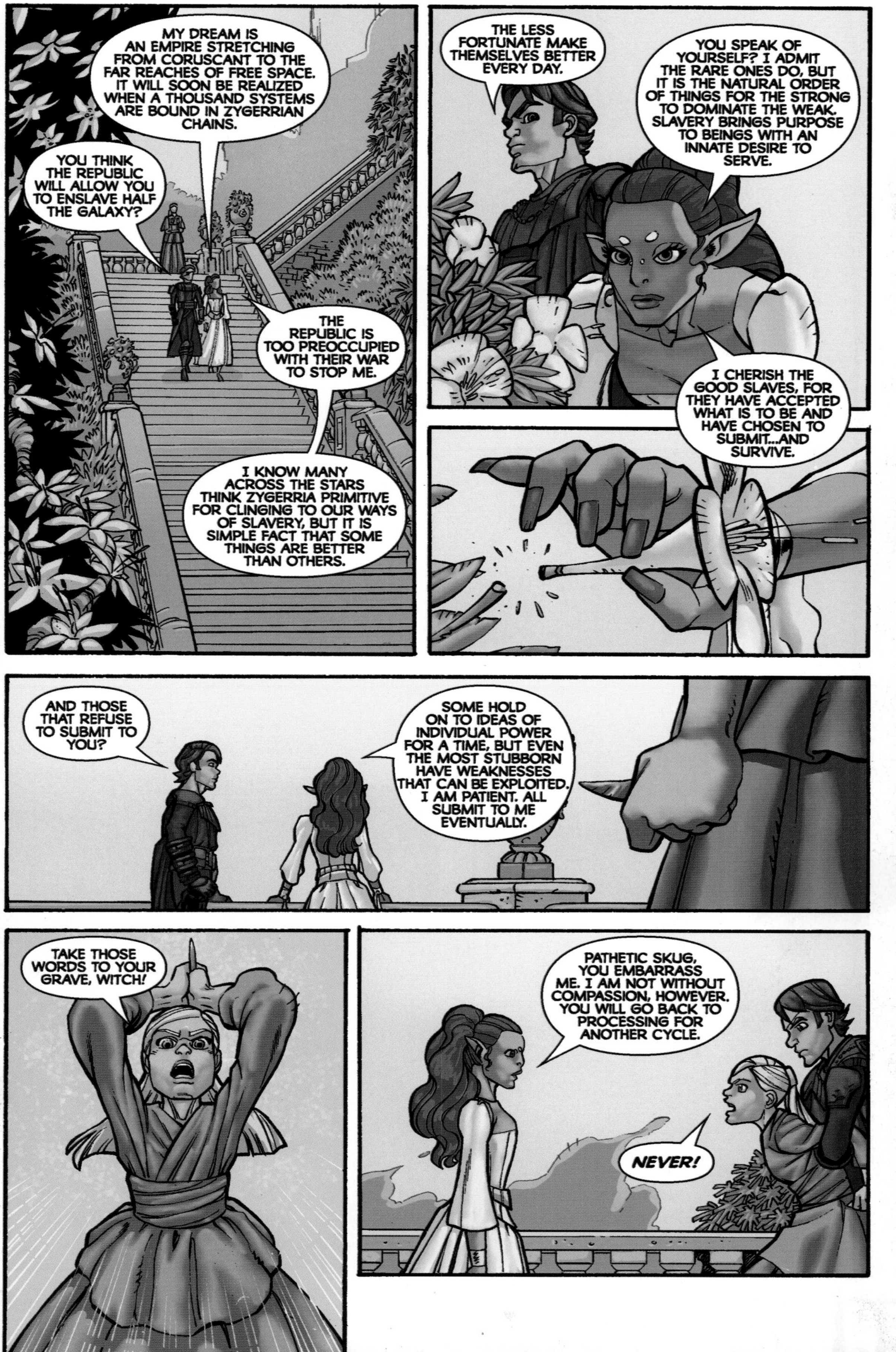
MY DREAM IS AN EMPIRE STRETCHING FROM CORUSCANT TO THE FAR REACHES OF FREE SPACE. IT WILL SOON BE REALIZED WHEN A THOUSAND SYSTEMS ARE BOUND IN ZYGERRIAN CHAINS.
YOU THINK THE REPUBLIC WILL ALLOW YOU TO ENSLAVE HALF THE GALAXY?
THE REPUBLIC IS TOO PREOCCUPIED WITH THEIR WAR TO STOP ME.
I KNOW MANY ACROSS THE STARS THINK ZYGERRIA PRIMITIVE FOR CLINGING TO OUR WAYS OF SLAVERY, BUT IT IS SIMPLE FACT THAT SOME THINGS ARE BETTER THAN OTHERS.
THE LESS FORTUNATE MAKE THEMSELVES BETTER EVERY DAY.
YOU SPEAK OF YOURSELF? I ADMIT THE RARE ONES DO, BUT IT IS THE NATURAL ORDER OF THINGS FOR THE STRONG TO DOMINATE THE WEAK. SLAVERY BRINGS PURPOSE TO BEINGS WITH AN INNATE DESIRE TO SERVE.
I CHERISH THE GOOD SLAVES, FOR THEY HAVE ACCEPTED WHAT IS TO BE AND HAVE CHOSEN TO SUBMIT...AND SURVIVE.
AND THOSE THAT REFUSE TO SUBMIT TO YOU?
SOME HOLD ON TO IDEAS OF INDIVIDUAL POWER FOR A TIME, BUT EVEN THE MOST STUBBORN HAVE WEAKNESSES THAT CAN BE EXPLOITED. I AM PATIENT. ALL SUBMIT TO ME EVENTUALLY.
TAKE THOSE WORDS TO YOUR GRAVE, WITCH!
PATHETIC SKUG, YOU EMBARRASS ME. I AM NOT WITHOUT COMPASSION, HOWEVER. YOU WILL GO BACK TO PROCESSING FOR ANOTHER CYCLE.
NEVER!

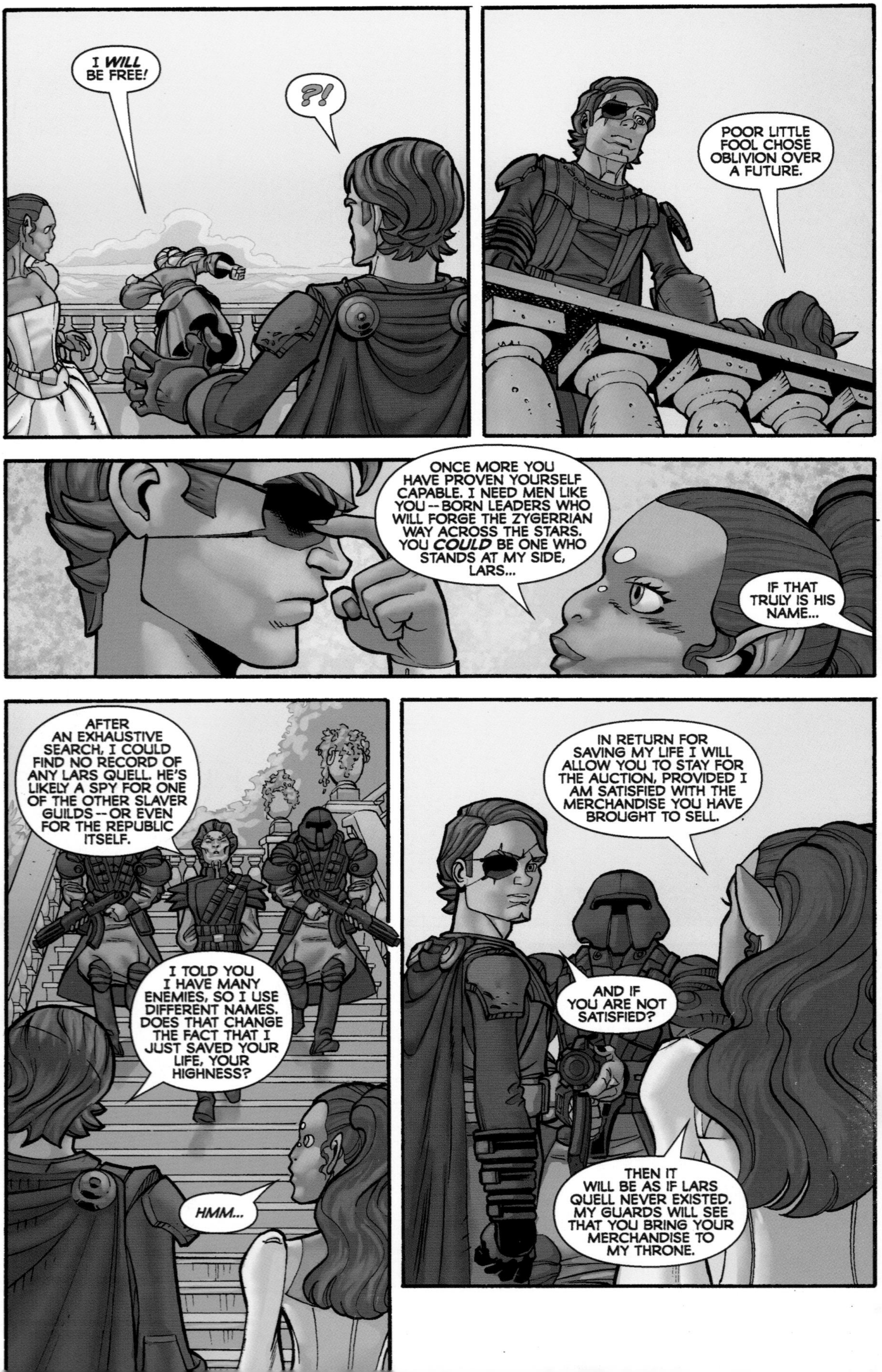

I WILL BE FREE!
?!
POOR LITTLE FOOL CHOSE OBLIVION OVER A FUTURE.
ONCE MORE YOU HAVE PROVEN YOURSELF CAPABLE. I NEED MEN LIKE YOU -- BORN LEADERS WHO WILL FORGE THE ZYGERRIAN WAY ACROSS THE STARS. YOU COULD BE ONE WHO STANDS AT MY SIDE, LARS...
IF THAT TRULY IS HIS NAME...
AFTER AN EXHAUSTIVE SEARCH, I COULD FIND NO RECORD OF ANY LARS QUELL. HE'S LIKELY A SPY FOR ONE OF THE OTHER SLAVER GUILDS -- OR EVEN FOR THE REPUBLIC ITSELF.
I TOLD YOU I HAVE MANY ENEMIES, SO I USE DIFFERENT NAMES. DOES THAT CHANGE THE FACT THAT I JUST SAVED YOUR LIFE, YOUR HIGHNESS?
HMM...
IN RETURN FOR SAVING MY LIFE I WILL ALLOW YOU TO STAY FOR THE AUCTION, PROVIDED I AM SATISFIED WITH THE MERCHANDISE YOU HAVE BROUGHT TO SELL.
AND IF YOU ARE NOT SATISFIED?
THEN IT WILL BE AS IF LARS QUELL NEVER EXISTED. MY GUARDS WILL SEE THAT YOU BRING YOUR MERCHANDISE TO MY THRONE.

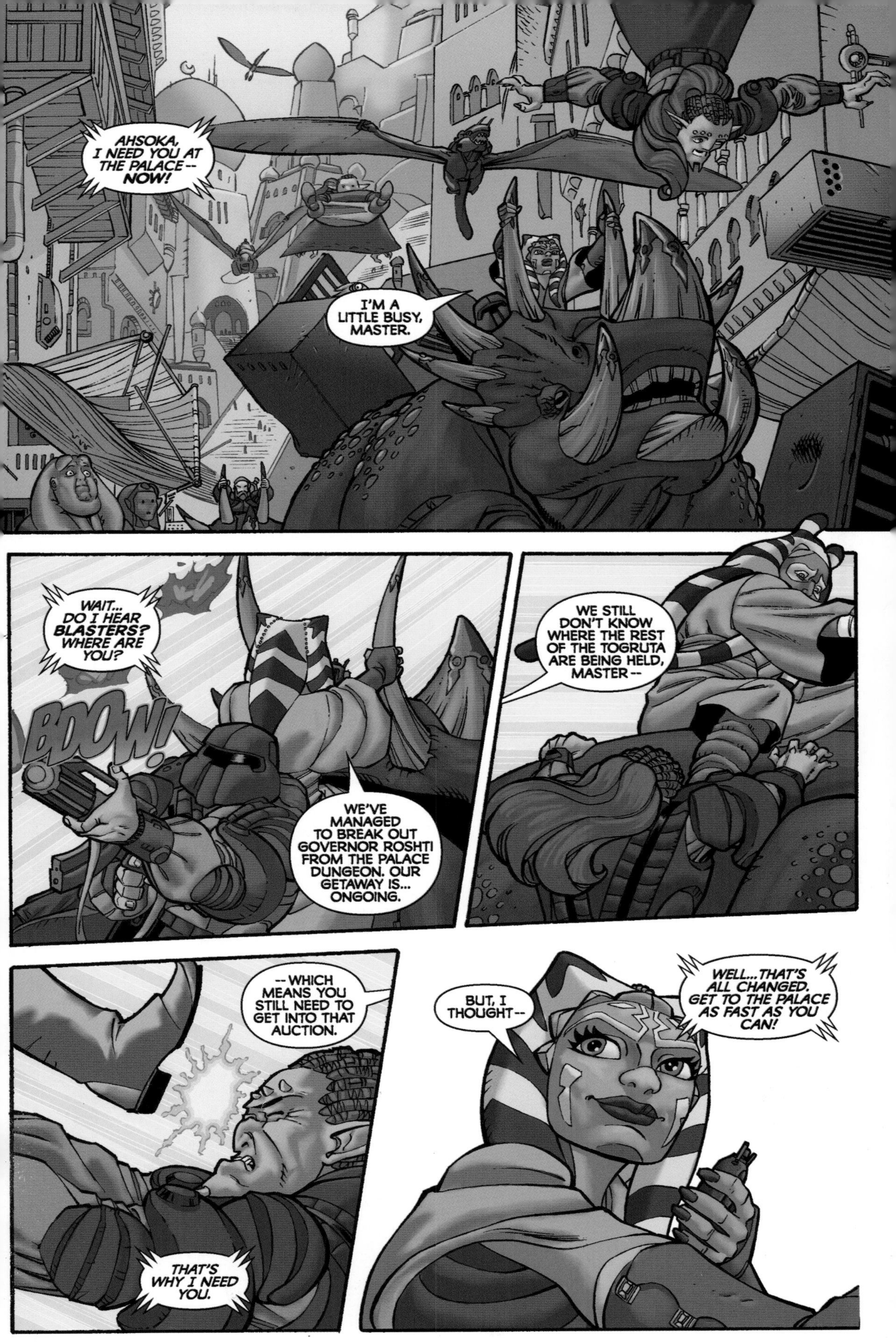
AHSOKA, I NEED YOU AT THE PALACE -- NOW!
I'M A LITTLE BUSY, MASTER.
WAIT... DO I HEAR BLASTERS? WHERE ARE YOU?
BDOW!
WE'VE MANAGED TO BREAK OUT GOVERNOR ROSHTI FROM THE PALACE DUNGEON. OUR GETAWAY IS... ONGOING.
WE STILL DON'T KNOW WHERE THE REST OF THE TOGRUTA ARE BEING HELD, MASTER --
-- WHICH MEANS YOU STILL NEED TO GET INTO THAT AUCTION.
THAT'S WHY I NEED YOU.
BUT, I THOUGHT--
WELL...THAT'S ALL CHANGED. GET TO THE PALACE AS FAST AS YOU CAN!

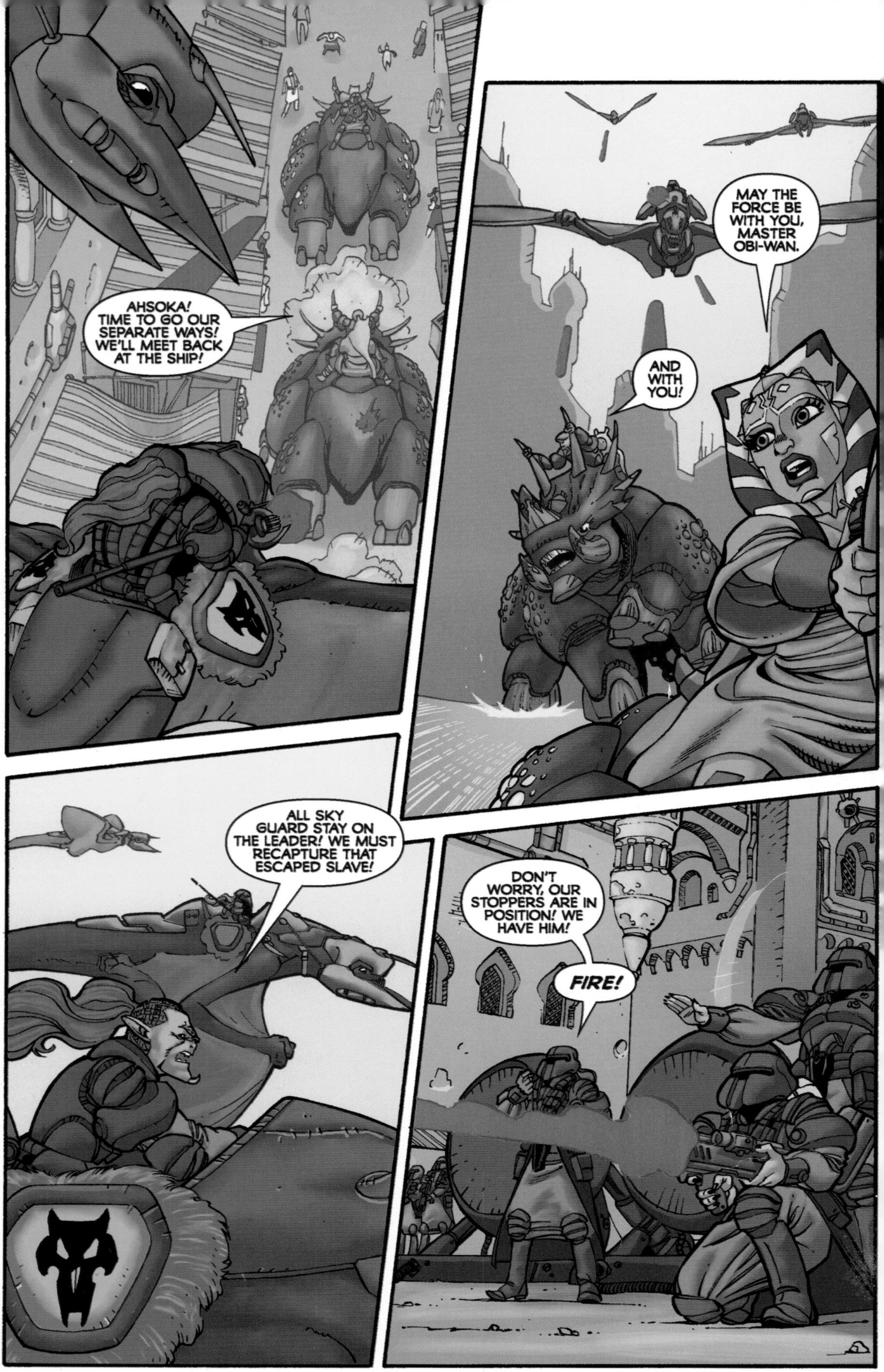
AHSOKA! TIME TO GO OUR SEPARATE WAYS! WE'LL MEET BACK AT THE SHIP!
MAY THE FORCE BE WITH YOU, MASTER OBI-WAN.
AND WITH YOU!
ALL SKY GUARD STAY ON THE LEADER! WE MUST RECAPTURE THAT ESCAPED SLAVE!
DON'T WORRY, OUR STOPPERS ARE IN POSITION! WE HAVE HIM!
FIRE!

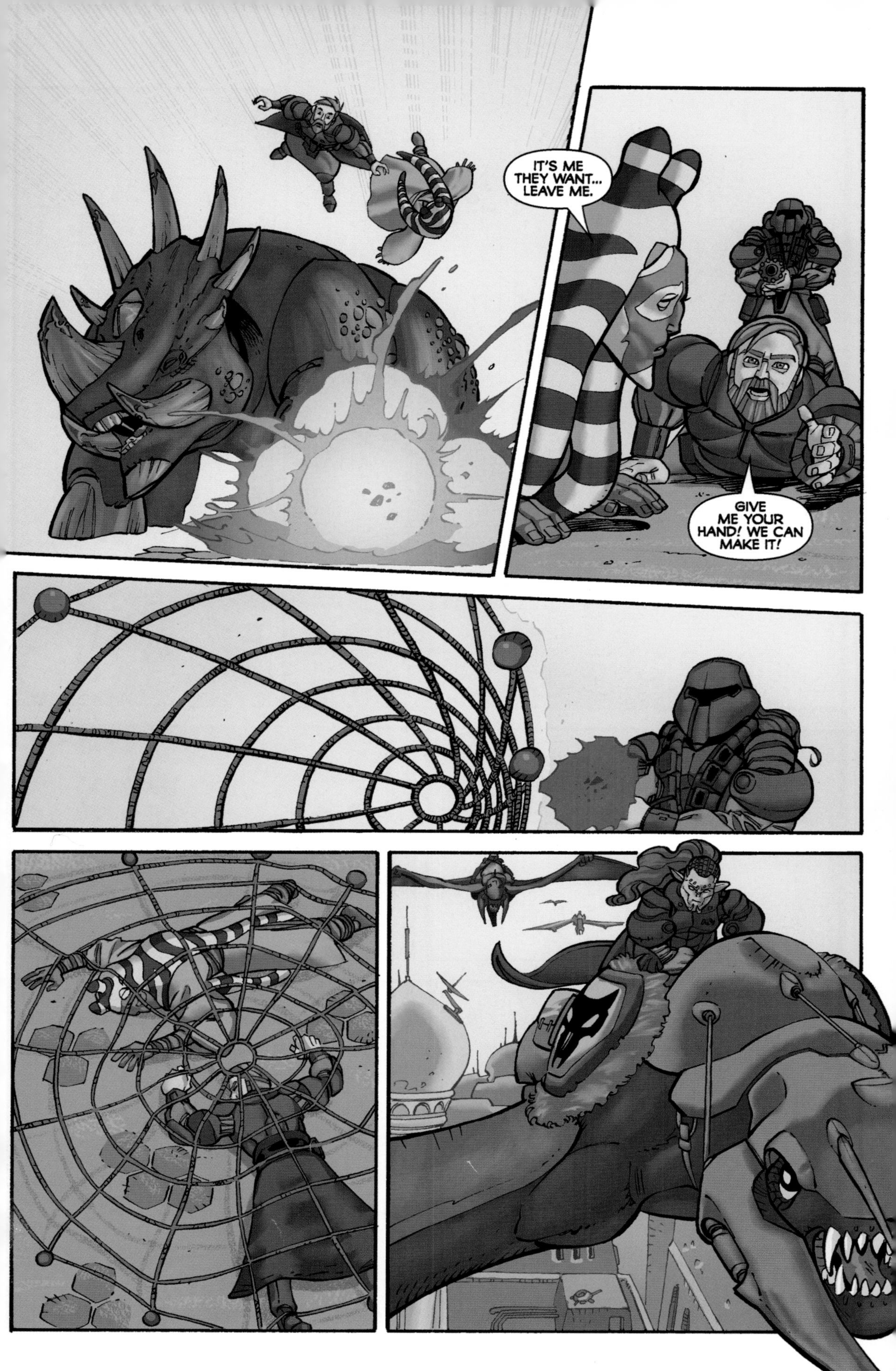
IT'S ME THEY WANT... LEAVE ME.
GIVE ME YOUR HAND! WE CAN MAKE IT!

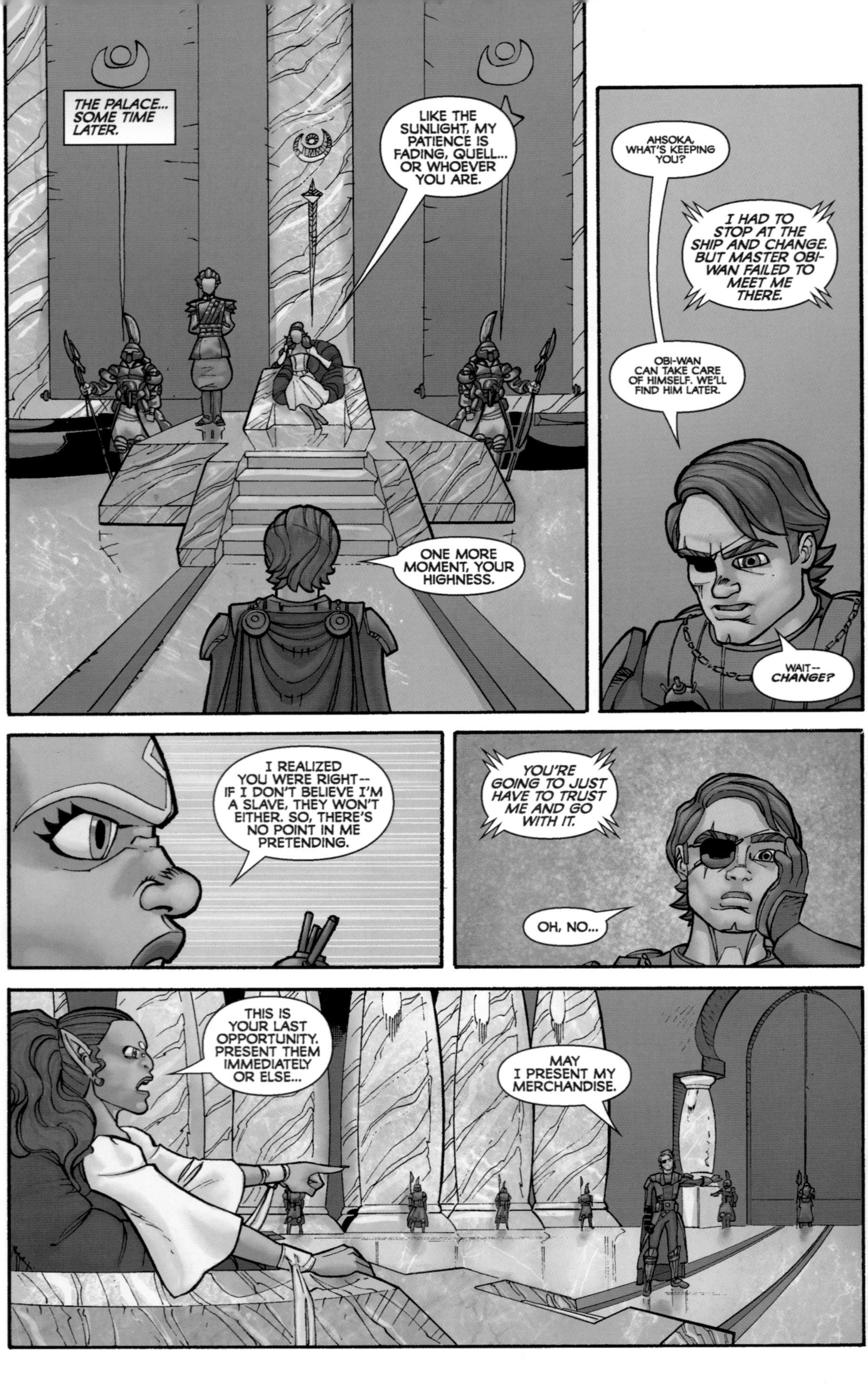
THE PALACE... SOME TIME LATER.
LIKE THE SUNLIGHT, MY PATIENCE IS FADING, QUELL... OR WHOEVER YOU ARE.
ONE MORE MOMENT, YOUR HIGHNESS.
AHSOKA, WHAT'S KEEPING YOU?
I HAD TO STOP AT THE SHIP AND CHANGE. BUT MASTER OBI-WAN FAILED TO MEET ME THERE.
OBI-WAN CAN TAKE CARE OF HIMSELF. WE'LL FIND HIM LATER.
WAIT-- CHANGE?
I REALIZED YOU WERE RIGHT-- IF I DON'T BELIEVE I'M A SLAVE, THEY WON'T EITHER. SO, THERE'S NO POINT IN ME PRETENDING.
YOU'RE GOING TO JUST HAVE TO TRUST ME AND GO WITH IT.
OH, NO...
THIS IS YOUR LAST OPPORTUNITY. PRESENT THEM IMMEDIATELY OR ELSE...
MAY I PRESENT MY MERCHANDISE.

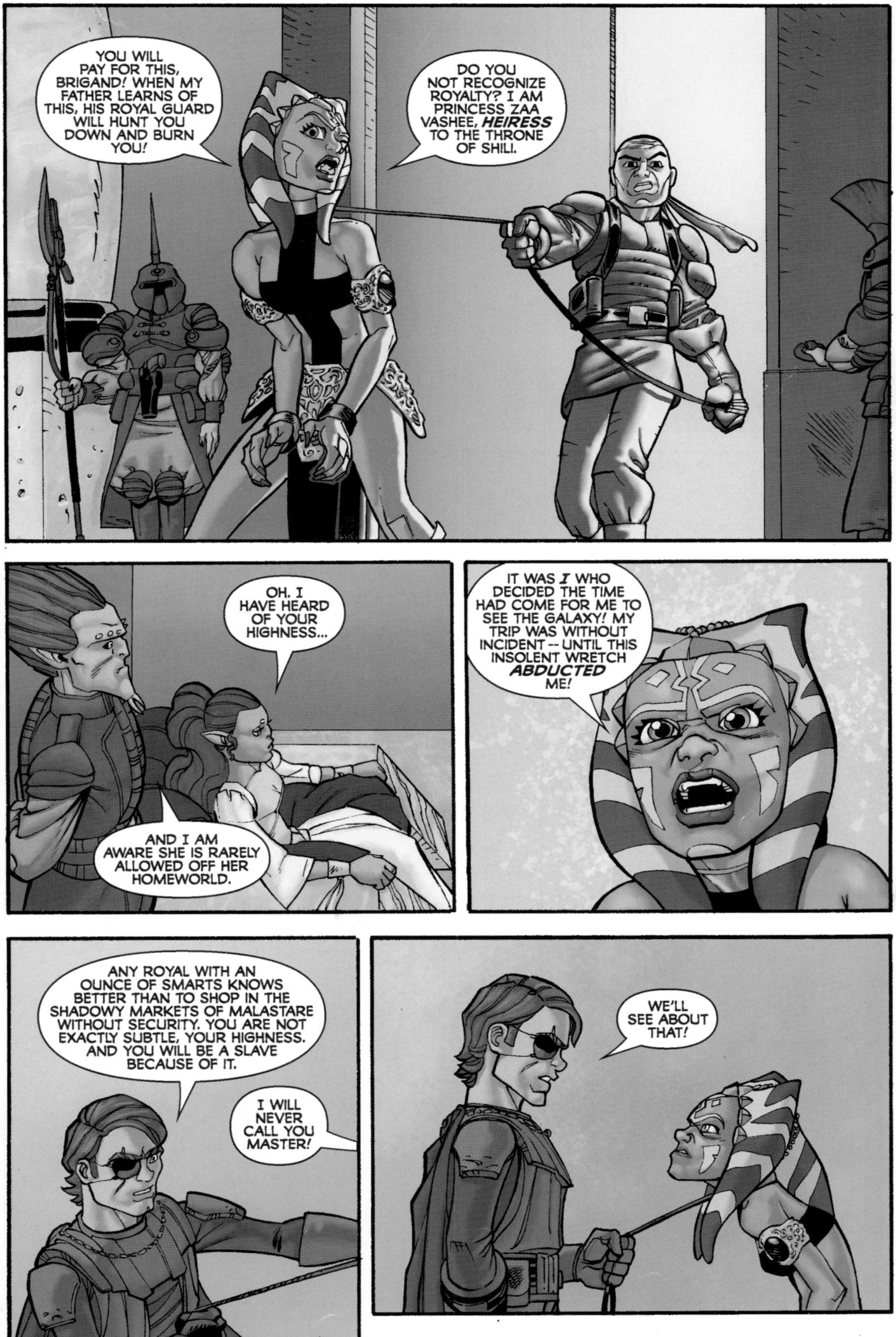
YOU WILL PAY FOR THIS, BRIGAND! WHEN MY FATHER LEARNS OF THIS, HIS ROYAL GUARD WILL HUNT YOU DOWN AND BURN YOU!
DO YOU NOT RECOGNIZE ROYALTY? I AM PRINCESS ZAA VASHEE, *HEIRESS* TO THE THRONE OF SHILI.
OH. I HAVE HEARD OF YOUR HIGHNESS...
AND I AM AWARE SHE IS RARELY ALLOWED OFF HER HOMEWORLD.
IT WAS *I* WHO DECIDED THE TIME HAD COME FOR ME TO SEE THE GALAXY! MY TRIP WAS WITHOUT INCIDENT -- UNTIL THIS INSOLENT WRETCH *ABDUCTED* ME!
ANY ROYAL WITH AN OUNCE OF SMARTS KNOWS BETTER THAN TO SHOP IN THE SHADOWY MARKETS OF MALASTARE WITHOUT SECURITY. YOU ARE NOT EXACTLY SUBTLE, YOUR HIGHNESS. AND YOU WILL BE A SLAVE BECAUSE OF IT.
I WILL NEVER CALL YOU MASTER!
WE'LL SEE ABOUT THAT!

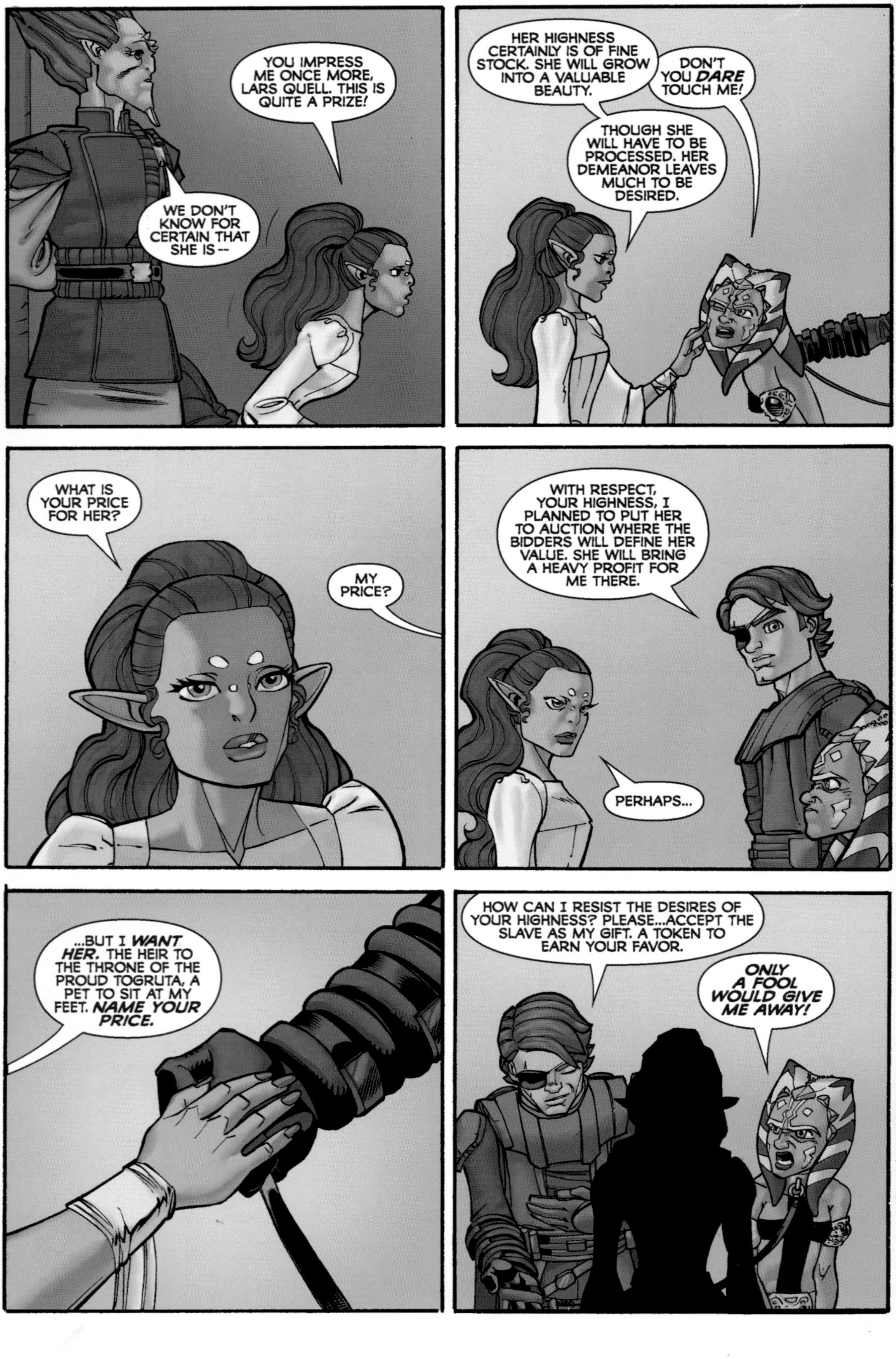

YOU IMPRESS ME ONCE MORE, LARS QUELL. THIS IS QUITE A PRIZE!
WE DON'T KNOW FOR CERTAIN THAT SHE IS--
HER HIGHNESS CERTAINLY IS OF FINE STOCK. SHE WILL GROW INTO A VALUABLE BEAUTY.
DON'T YOU *DARE* TOUCH ME!
THOUGH SHE WILL HAVE TO BE PROCESSED. HER DEMEANOR LEAVES MUCH TO BE DESIRED.
WHAT IS YOUR PRICE FOR HER?
MY PRICE?
WITH RESPECT, YOUR HIGHNESS, I PLANNED TO PUT HER TO AUCTION WHERE THE BIDDERS WILL DEFINE HER VALUE. SHE WILL BRING A HEAVY PROFIT FOR ME THERE.
PERHAPS...
...BUT I *WANT HER.* THE HEIR TO THE THRONE OF THE PROUD TOGRUTA, A PET TO SIT AT MY FEET. ***NAME YOUR PRICE.***
HOW CAN I RESIST THE DESIRES OF YOUR HIGHNESS? PLEASE...ACCEPT THE SLAVE AS MY GIFT. A TOKEN TO EARN YOUR FAVOR.
ONLY A FOOL WOULD GIVE ME AWAY!

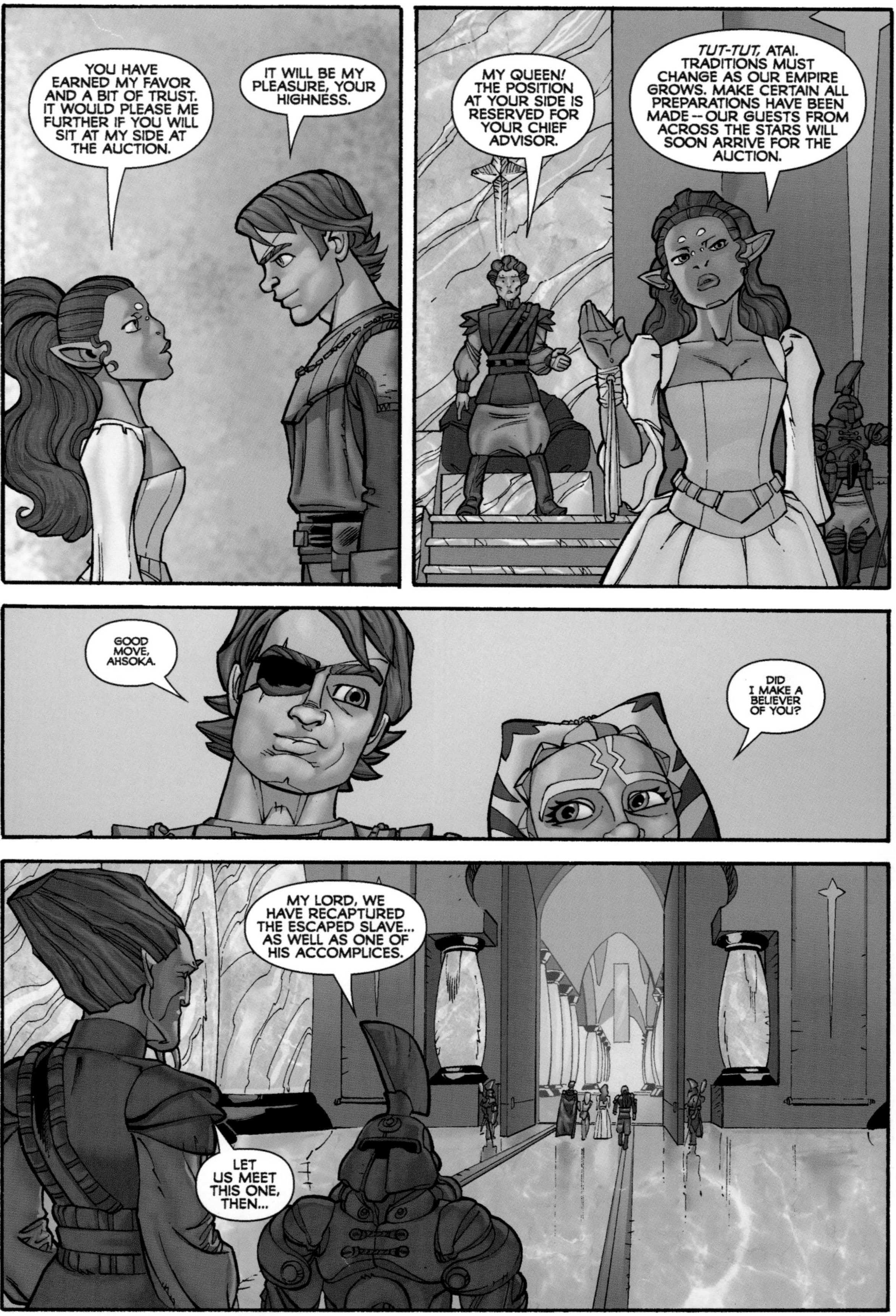
YOU HAVE EARNED MY FAVOR AND A BIT OF TRUST. IT WOULD PLEASE ME FURTHER IF YOU WILL SIT AT MY SIDE AT THE AUCTION.
IT WILL BE MY PLEASURE, YOUR HIGHNESS.
MY QUEEN! THE POSITION AT YOUR SIDE IS RESERVED FOR YOUR CHIEF ADVISOR.
TUT-TUT, ATAI. TRADITIONS MUST CHANGE AS OUR EMPIRE GROWS. MAKE CERTAIN ALL PREPARATIONS HAVE BEEN MADE -- OUR GUESTS FROM ACROSS THE STARS WILL SOON ARRIVE FOR THE AUCTION.
GOOD MOVE, AHSOKA.
DID I MAKE A BELIEVER OF YOU?
MY LORD, WE HAVE RECAPTURED THE ESCAPED SLAVE... AS WELL AS ONE OF HIS ACCOMPLICES.
LET US MEET THIS ONE, THEN...

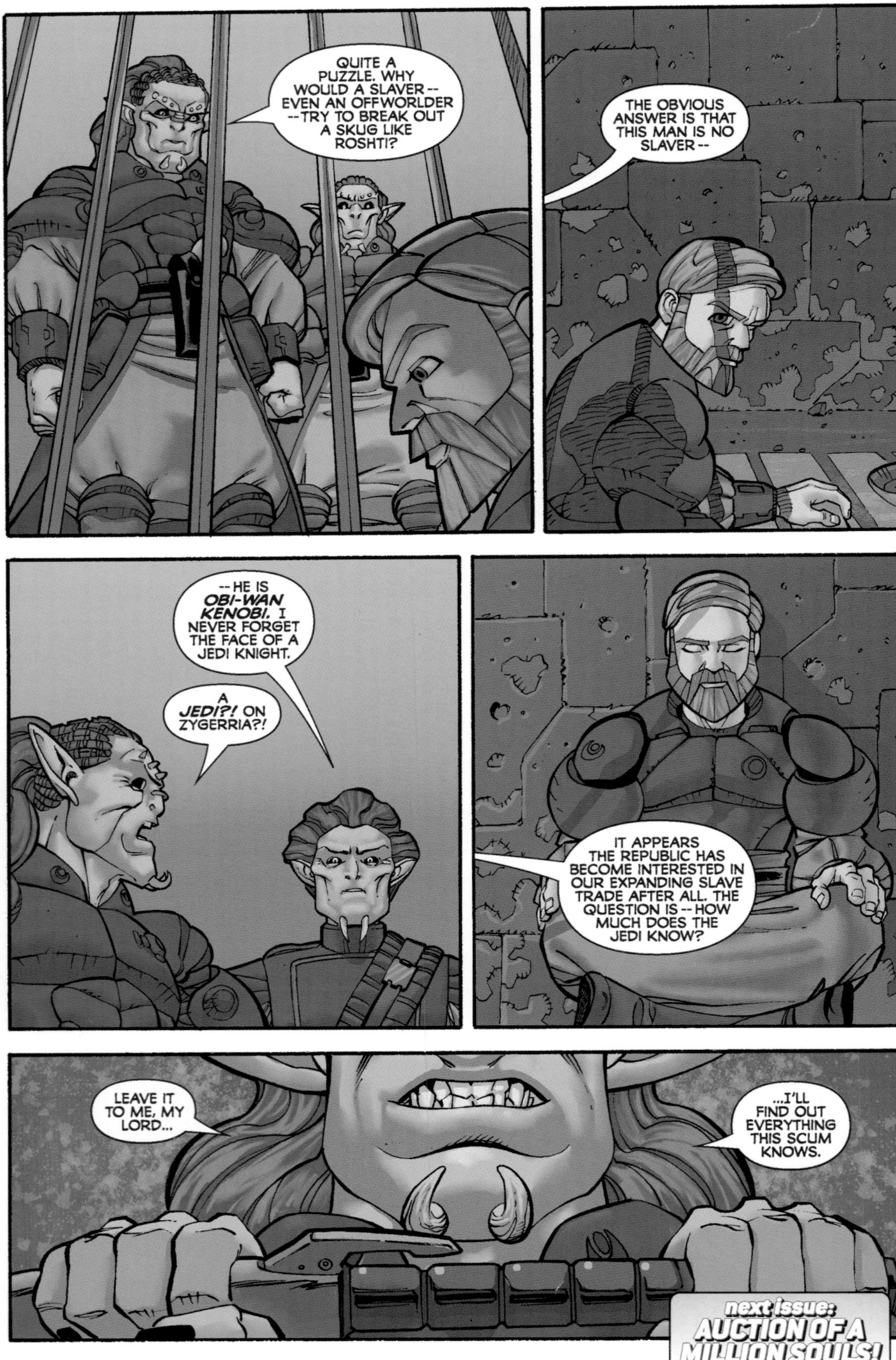
QUITE A PUZZLE. WHY WOULD A SLAVER -- EVEN AN OFFWORLDER -- TRY TO BREAK OUT A SKUG LIKE ROSHTI?
THE OBVIOUS ANSWER IS THAT THIS MAN IS NO SLAVER --
-- HE IS *OBI-WAN KENOBI.* I NEVER FORGET THE FACE OF A JEDI KNIGHT.
A *JEDI?!* ON ZYGERRIA?!
IT APPEARS THE REPUBLIC HAS BECOME INTERESTED IN OUR EXPANDING SLAVE TRADE AFTER ALL. THE QUESTION IS -- HOW MUCH DOES THE JEDI KNOW?
LEAVE IT TO ME, MY LORD...
...I'LL FIND OUT EVERYTHING THIS SCUM KNOWS.
next issue:
AUCTION OF A MILLION SOULS!